2017 xoxo

To Avery and Emma,
Thank you for choosing
words of kindness.
It matters!
Love,
Lauren
Garretson
♡

1

3

Willamena Picklepants

and a Case of the No-Good, Really Mean Words

by Lauri Garretson

illustrated by Yulia Quomariah

WILLAMENA PICKLEPANTS
WORDS MATTER & KINDNESS COUNTS

www.lifeisastorybook.com

Kidlit to Book
www.kidlittobook.com

Willamena Picklepants / Lauri Garretson
ISBN-13: 978-1-945793-01-1
ISBN-10: 1-945793-01-5

For my 4 L's and my 1 T.

And for all the Willamenas in this world ...
may you remember words matter and kindness counts!

Willamena Picklepants is a girl I once knew,
With her goldfish named Bubbles
and her bulldog named Blue.
High-top sneakers, floppy pigtails, and a welcoming grin
Spotted freckles on her cheeks, and a dimple on her chin.

Willamena Picklepants was an ordinary kid
With one problem that stunk — yes it certainly did!
Her name was unusual and difficult to spell,
It made her so embarrassed
that she wanted to yell!

So Miss Picklepants one morning did declare:
"My name is ridiculous—it's terribly unfair!
I will cross my fingers and wish with all my might:
I'll have a brand new name by tomorrow night!

A name that is normal and easy to say,
A name that is common; one you hear every day
Like Lauren or Lizzy or Lucy or Lily,
Not a name like Willamena that sounds super silly!"

Then the school bell did ring as the clock struck ten.
It was time for recess—that time once again.
Off to the playground the kids scurried on their way.
Willamena sure did dread this part of her day.

The kids in a circle, they were playing a game,
Laughing and giggling as they chanted her name.

With tears in her eyes and her heart nearly breaking
She ran as fast as she could from the mess they were making.
Those words were unkind; they were mean—that is true.
They hurt and they stung and left her feeling quite blue.

With her head hanging low she sure wanted to cry.
"Kids can be mean!" she exclaimed with a sigh.
Then off of the monkey bars her old friend did land
With words of wisdom and a well thought-out plan.

"Willamena, Willamena, you really must know,
Words are like seeds: We reap what we sow.

You're more than your name—
it's only one part.

What makes you **unique** comes
from deep in your **heart**.

"Those words that were spoken,
they were mean, that's a fact.
But **you** get to **choose**. How will you react?
Will you repeat the cycle with mean words and hate?
Or be strong—a leader—and refuse to participate?

"Willamena, here's the lesson, and it's very good news!
You must decide—yes, you get to choose.
Will you speak words that are loving and kind?
Or will you cause pain—is that what others will find?"
We all get to choose to harm or to heal.
The words that we speak are **powerful** and **real**."

Willamena is a hero, that's something you must know.
This story isn't sad, that's not how things should go.
Willamena was stronger than those kids ever knew.

She brushed the words off and knew just what to do.
She made a brave choice, pushed her old thoughts aside.
Her heart felt better; she didn't need to hide.

(I'll bet she was nervous, I'm not gonna lie).

She marched toward those kids with her shoulders held high.

Then she told them what she'd learned and how much it mattered.
They had hurt her heart, but it wouldn't stay shattered.

"Willamena is my name and I want you to know...

"The things that you said had me feeling quite low.

"I'm more than my name with feelings and a heart,
Those words that you spoke, they tear friends apart.
Yes, my name is unusual and difficult to spell,

But I am who
I am and
I think
I'm quite
SWELL!"

"So there you have it —
you've heard it here today.
I hope you'll consider it; I hope you'll obey.

"Our words are important,
I officially declare!
The world needs more love,
more kindness and care.
Yes, I'll say it out loud with
a strong, booming voice:
Willamena is my name —
and kind words are my choice!"

"Grace draws a circle around
everyone and says they're in."
- Bob Goff

Proverbs 12:18

words
have
power

Made in the USA
San Bernardino, CA
20 August 2017